The Kingdom of Wrenly

14

A Ghost in the Castle

By Jordan Quinn

Illustrated by Robert McPhillips

LITTLE SIMON

New York   London   Toronto   Sydney   New Delhi

LITTLE SIMON

An imprint of Simon & Schuster Children's Publishing Division
1230 Avenue of the Americas, New York, New York 10020
First Little Simon paperback edition June 2019
Copyright © 2019 by Simon & Schuster, Inc.
Also available in a Little Simon hardcover edition.
All rights reserved, including the right of reproduction in whole or in part in any form.
LITTLE SIMON is a registered trademark of Simon & Schuster, Inc., and associated colophon is a trademark of Simon & Schuster, Inc.
For information about special discounts for bulk purchases, please contact
Simon & Schuster Special Sales at 1-866-506-1949 or business@simonandschuster.com.
The Simon & Schuster Speakers Bureau can bring authors to your live event. For more information or to book an event contact the Simon & Schuster Speakers Bureau
at 1-866-248-3049 or visit our website at www.simonspeakers.com.
Manufactured in the United States of America 0820 MTN
4 6 8 10 9 7 5 3
This book has been cataloged with the Library of Congress.
ISBN 978-1-5344-4511-6 (hc)
ISBN 978-1-5344-4510-9 (pbk)
ISBN 978-1-5344-4512-3 (eBook)

CONTENTS

CHAPTER 1

Bumps in
the Night

Ooooooooooo . . . !

OOOOOOOOOO . . . !

Creeeeeeak!

The door to Prince Lucas's room
whined as it opened. A wave of cold
air swept into his chamber. Ruskin,
Lucas's pet scarlet dragon, lifted
his ears. Then—*CLUMP!* The door
banged shut in the darkness. Lucas
gasped and sat straight up in bed.

"What was *that*?" he whispered, staring at the closed door. Ruskin shook his head and whimpered.

The prince looked at the moon shimmering on the water outside the palace. His curtains blew gently in the breeze.

"It must have been a gust of wind," the prince reasoned. But just as he said this, the strange, spooky sound began again.

Ooooooooooo . . . !

OOOOOOOOOO . . . !

Ruskin jumped onto Lucas's bed.

"Somebody's awake," Lucas said softly. "Let's go find out who it is." The prince slid out of bed, and Ruskin followed.

The prince slowly opened the door. The light from the moon was just enough for him to see down the passageway. They tiptoed through the first arch. Then they heard the eerie wail again.

Oooooooooo . . . !

OOOOOOOOOO . . . !

Ruskin scrambled and hid beside a decorative suit of armor. His head peeked out.

Lucas smiled nervously. "Would you believe me if I said that was probably just the wind too?" Lucas whispered to his dragon.

The wind often whistled through the palace on stormy nights. Only tonight wasn't stormy. And the sound was definitely a moan—not a whistle.

"Come on, Ruskin," the prince said. "I'd really like to know who's making these creepy noises."

The two of them crept down the hall and peered around the corner. At the end of the next passageway, they saw a glowing bluish light.

As they tiptoed closer to the light, the air turned ice cold. Lucas hugged himself to keep warm.

If these are winds, then they are blowing in from Flatfrost tonight, he thought. Then he gulped at the ridiculous thought. It was summer in Wrenly, after all.

Slowly a shadow stretched across the wall at the end of the passageway. It had long bony fingers and a tall pointed hat. Lucas and Ruskin froze. Then the shadowy somebody came into view.

Lucas gasped. It was André—one of the kingdom's top wizards.

"What are you two doing up?" the wizard asked.

Ruskin looked at Lucas, who did all the talking. "We heard strange noises and came to see who it was."

André frowned. "Well, now you know," he said gruffly. "Get along back to bed. Sleep is important for young princes . . . and their curious dragons."

Lucas nodded as a wave of relief washed over him. The spooky noises had only been André all along. But what was he doing wandering the halls at this late hour?

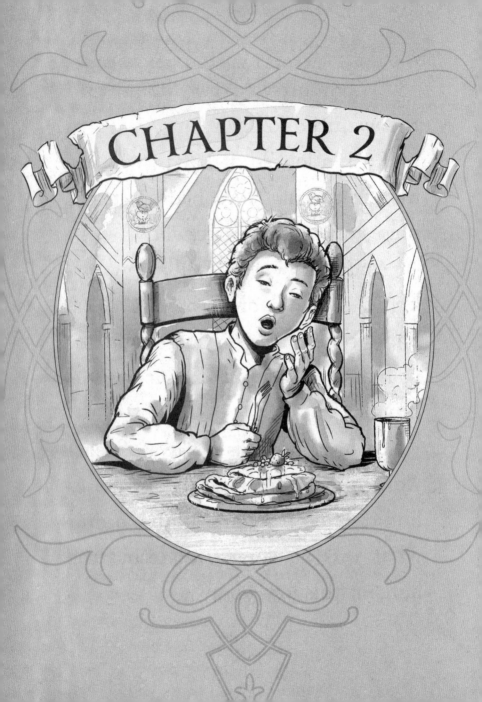

Dragon Hound

Lucas yawned over his pancakes.

"What's up, sleepyhead?" asked his best friend, Clara. She had come to the castle early with her mother, who worked for Queen Tasha.

Lucas rubbed his eyes and sat up in his chair. "Ruskin and I had a *late* night," he said.

Clara sat down at the table. "How come?"

Lucas told Clara all about the weird sounds, the mysterious chill in the hallway, the glowing light, and bumping into André.

"Wow," Clara said. "That *does* sound creepy, though Ruskin doesn't seem nearly as tired as you."

The dragon was busy scratching and sniffing at one of the dining room doors.

"Ruskin, no!" the prince scolded. He didn't want the young dragon getting in trouble with his parents.

Ruskin listened to his friend and stopped scratching but kept sniffing at the door.

Clara stood and walked over to Ruskin. "He really wants whatever is behind here."

In one smooth move, Clara pulled the handle and Ruskin escaped through the opening.

Lucas leaped up. He was wide awake now. "What is it?"

Clara peered down the hallway as a blue light disappeared around a corner. "The glowing light—it's back! And Ruskin chased after it!"

Lucas quickly charged into the hall with Clara right behind him. Soon they caught sight of Ruskin's tail flying around the next bend. Then they lost sight of him again. Every time they caught a glimpse of the dragon, he'd disappear down

another hallway, chasing after the light.

"This castle goes on forever' Clara shouted.

Lucas yelled over his shoulder. "Don't worry. There's a dead end coming up."

Sure enough, Ruskin was waiting at the dead end. The dragon sat in a heap, rubbing his head and squawking at the wall. The last of the glowing mist seeped through the wall and was gone.

"Whoa! Did you see *that*?" Clara exclaimed, her eyes round with wonder. "What was that?"

Lucas touched the cold, hard stones.

"I don't know," he said. "But whatever it was, it just went through a solid wall."

CHAPTER 3

Seeing Things

Clara tried to make sense of what they had just seen.

"Perhaps our eyes were playing tricks on us," she suggested.

Lucas sighed as they walked back down the hall. "Maybe it's because we haven't eaten breakfast."

Clara's stomach agreed, letting out a loud rumble, which made both of the friends laugh.

"Are you hungry too, Ruskin?" the prince asked.

Ruskin growled and looked back down the passageway. He was more interested in what he'd been chasing than in food.

The kids hurried into the royal kitchen.

"Good morning, Cook," Lucas said. "We're really hungry."

Cook turned around from a pot of soup he'd been stirring.

"I *just* threw out your untouched pancakes!" he grumbled. "If you want something to eat, you'll have to fetch it yourself."

Lucas and Clara had no trouble finding food. They grabbed yogurt, fruit, bread, and butter. As they carried their breakfast to the kitchen table, they heard Cook whistle for Ruskin.

"Here, boy!" he called. "I saved you a nice juicy bone!"

Ruskin scampered after Cook as he left the room.

"Hopefully, this food will cure us of seeing things," Lucas said as the kids sat down at the table.

No sooner had Lucas spoken these words than a strange woman appeared in the kitchen. She had long, wavy white hair and a misty gray-blue dress. She looked pale as if she hadn't been outside in a very long time.

"Can we help you?" Lucas asked.

The woman drew closer. Her dress floated behind her, and the air around her felt cold. Lucas got goose bumps.

"Yes," said the woman in a voice that was strange and distant. "Tell me about your dragon."

Lucas set down his yogurt on the table. Although there was something odd about this woman, his biggest fear was that Ruskin had gotten into trouble.

"Okay, what did he do now?" the prince asked. "Did he scorch something that belonged to you?"

The woman shook her head. "No," she said with a long whispered o. "I just want to know how he came to live in the castle."

Lucas smiled. He didn't mind telling the story of how Ruskin had come to live with him. It was his favorite tale. He told the pale woman about the discovery of a scarlet dragon egg, how it had hatched, and how Ruskin had been given to him by his father, King Caleb.

Clara spoke of the baby dragon's illness and the cure they had found just in time.

Soon the two friends were so wrapped up in their stories that

they didn't notice Cook and Ruskin
return to the kitchen.

"Who are you talking to?" Cook
asked. The children looked up.

"We're talking to your friend," Lucas said, but when the prince looked back at the woman, she was gone. "Wait, she was here a moment ago."

"Someone was in my kitchen?" Cook asked.

Lucas described the woman who had been talking with them. "A pale woman," he said, "with a flowing dress and long white hair."

"And a weird, echoey voice," Clara added.

Cook raised an eyebrow, and then he laughed.

"You're putting me on!" he said.
"You sure have wild imaginations!
A pale woman with a weird, echoey
voice in my kitchen. Hilarious."

The kids' mouths both dropped
open. They weren't playing a joke.

The woman had been there. Lucas and Clara had both seen and talked to her.

Cook stood back and studied their faces. "My goodness! You look as if you'd just seen a *ghost*!"

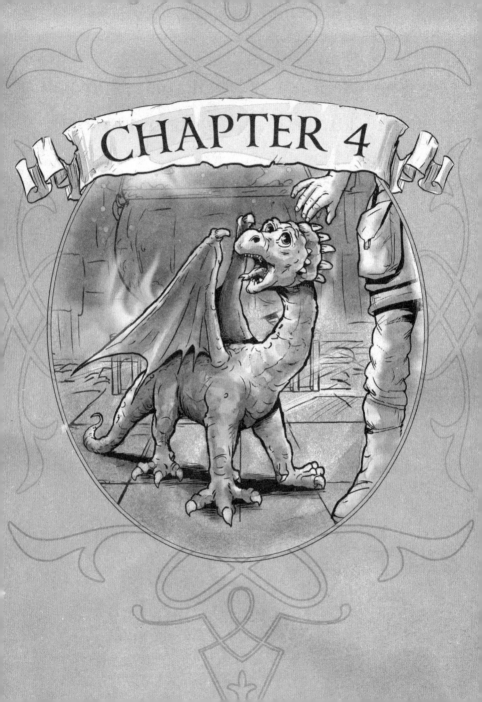

CHAPTER 4

A Mysterious Mission

"I wonder who that strange lady could be," Lucas said.

Clara shook her head. "I don't know, but we need to find out. What if she wants to rob the palace?"

Lucas gasped. "Or worse, steal Ruskin!"

Ruskin squawked at the thought.

"Don't worry, boy," said Clara. "You're safe with us."

The children had found a new adventure: Find the mysterious lady.

HAVE YOU SEEN THIS WOMAN?

They spent the day searching the castle. The first person they bumped into was a royal guard in the hallway. They described the pale lady to the guard.

The guard shook his head. "I've been on duty since four this morning," he said. "I haven't seen anyone who fits *that* description."

Next they moved on to the royal study, where Queen Tasha was reading.

"Excuse me, Mother," Lucas said. "Did you invite anyone to the palace today, like an older woman with long white hair?"

Queen Tasha set her book down
and chuckled. "Are you three on some
sort of imaginary adventure?"

The children sighed because the
queen wasn't taking them seriously.

"No, Your Highness. I'm afraid we are very serious," Clara said. "We saw a strange woman in the kitchen, and Cook said he didn't know who she was."

The queen thought for a moment, then shook her head. "Well, I promise I haven't invited anyone over today."

Lucas and Clara left the study and continued on their mission.

They climbed the back stairs to the upper floors of the castle. Then they roamed the hallways.

"Wait, I hear footsteps!" Lucas whispered.

The kids and Ruskin stepped behind a pillar as the footsteps came closer. Lucas peered out from behind their hiding spot.

"Look, it's André!" he whispered. "I wonder why he's patrolling these hallways again." Lucas stepped out slowly, and Clara and Ruskin followed.

"Hi!" the prince said casually.

André stopped and stared. "What is this, a game of hide-and-seek?"

Lucas brushed a cobweb from his arm. "Actually, maybe. We're *seeking* a woman. Have you seen anyone strange wandering the palace?"

"Only the three of you," André said with a touch of frost. "But tell me, what does this woman you speak of look like?"

Lucas and Clara described her.

André nodded as the children spoke. Then he asked, "What was she looking for?"

Lucas thought for a moment. "She asked about Ruskin."

The wizard stroked his beard thoughtfully. "Hmm . . . very interesting. And why do you think I would know something about this woman?"

Lucas shifted from one foot to the other. "Because *you're* the only one in the passageway, and we thought you might have seen her."

The wizard stuck out his chin and nodded slightly. "Did this woman happen to ask for me by name?"

Lucas wrinkled his brow. *What kind of weird question is that?* he wondered.

"No, she only mentioned Ruskin," said Clara.

André reached out and patted Ruskin on the back.

"I see," he said. "Well, I'm afraid I don't know anything about your mysterious woman. Now, shouldn't you two be at archery training?"

Lucas and Clara had forgotten all about their morning training. They thanked André and turned to leave. As they walked away, Lucas noticed the wizard hurry off in the other direction. And he was moving faster than Lucas had ever seen him move before.

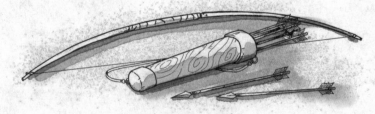

CHAPTER 5

Eavesdroppers

Lucas and Clara each collected a bow and quiver of arrows and set them down in the courtyard. Gray clouds rushed by overhead as they prepared their targets. Then they took turns aiming for the bull's-eye.

"That makes three out of six!" Lucas said proudly.

"Ha-ha! Four out of six for me!" Clara said.

Then they raced to the targets to collect the arrows. As the kids pulled out the arrows, they overheard one of the knights talking to his captain on the walkway above them.

"Captain, I've come to report some odd happenings in the castle," he said. Lucas and Clara stopped what they were doing and listened.

"What kind of odd happenings?" the captain asked.

The knight told his story in a hushed voice. "Well, when I was on my rounds in the West Turret, a wave of cold mist flooded the stairwell."

Lucas and Clara looked at each other with wide eyes.

The knight continued. "And as I moved into the passageway I heard somebody whispering, but nobody was there."

The captain cleared her throat and asked, "It's good that you brought this to me first. Have any of the other knights reported such happenings?"

The knight shifted nervously.

"They have, Captain," he said. "Many guards have reported hearing strange noises, and one swears he saw a woman *float through a wall*."

Lucas clamped Clara's arm.

"That's like what *we* saw!" he whispered. The color washed out of Lucas's and Clara's faces as the two friends listened for the captain's response.

"There has to be a logical reason for these events," she said. "But you must not speak of this again. We don't want to upset the royal family. This is a mystery the knights will solve *alone*."

"Yes, Captain."

Lucas ripped an arrow out of the target. "*We* need to solve this mystery."

Clara nodded. "And I know a good place to gather information."

A sly smile swept over Lucas's face because he knew they were thinking of the same place: the library.

THE ROYAL LIBRARY

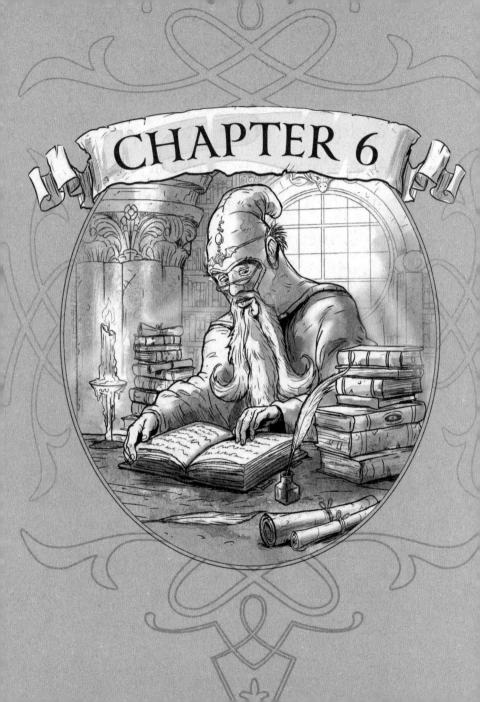

CHAPTER 6

Ghost Writer

Lucas, Clara, and Ruskin pushed through the polished double doors to the Royal Library and screeched to a stop. Sitting at one of the tables was André. The wizard looked up from his books, surprised to see them.

"What in Wrenly are *you* doing here?" André asked. "Wait. Are you following me?"

"No, we promise," said Lucas.

The wizard stood and fumbled to collect the books he was reading. He stuffed some into his satchel and gathered a few in his arms.

"If you need me, I'll be . . . well, I'll be far away from you two," André said, and he hurried past the children.

He struggled to balance the books in his arms and didn't notice one slip to the floor.

Lucas ran over and picked up the book. "Hey, André!" he called helpfully. "Hey! Hey, you dropped this!"

But André was already down the hall. With a shrug, Lucas walked back over to Clara.

"What book is it?" she asked.

Lucas read the gold writing on the cover. "It's called *The History of the Kingdom of Wrenly.*"

The children sat and studied the
table of contents. There were chapters
like: The Building of Wrenly Palace,
The Royal Families of Wrenly, and
The Battles of Wrenly.

"This sounds like an interesting chapter," Lucas said. "The Folklore of Wrenly."

They flipped through the pages to find the chapter on folklore. There were stories of sea serpents,

Sea Serpent

mermaids, unicorns, pegasi, griffins, basilisks, sirens, and more, but at the end of the list, someone had handwritten in one more creature.

"*Ghosts!*" they both said at the same time.

At the end of the chapter, they found a handwritten entry.

The Haunting of Wrenly Palace

It has been said that the ghost of a woman haunts the halls of Wrenly Palace. She can change form in an instant. One moment she seems solid and mortal, and the next she is nothing more than a glowing mist, able to pass through walls. In her presence, one might feel a striking drop in temperature. Sometimes her whispers and moans have been heard in the passageways. Then, one day, she disappeared and never returned.

Clara pointed to the name under the story. "Look who wrote this."

Lucas read the author's name and frowned. "It was Falsk."

Falsk was a fairy, but she was known in Wrenly as the False Fairy because she always stretched the truth too far. Even though Falsk had helped Lucas and Clara on an adventure once, many of her stories had been proven to be lies.

"But this story is true," Clara reminded the prince. "Everything in it has happened to us."

Lucas nodded. "And it happened to the royal knights, too."

Then something new caught Clara's eyes. Someone had written a note in the margin of the book. It said, *Tonight at midnight. West Turret. Empty Room.*

Lucas studied the words. "I wonder when this was written."

"The ink looks fresh," Clara said. "It smears when I run my finger over it." Clara held up her ink-stained finger.

"It looks like we have a date in the West Turret at the stroke of midnight," Lucas said. Then he added, "With a ghost."

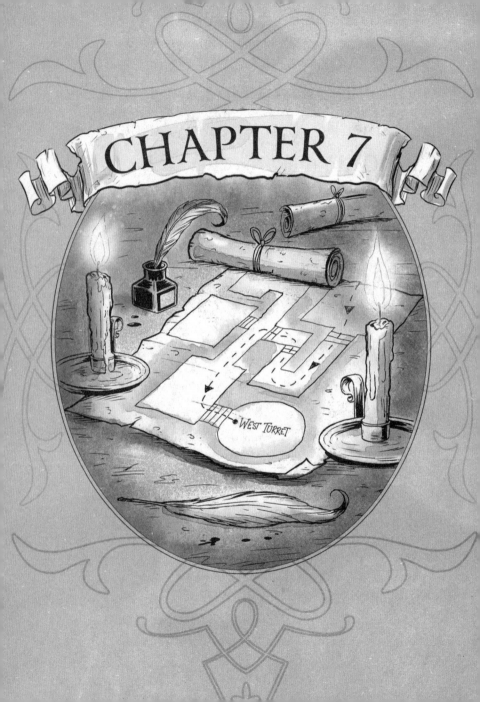

CHAPTER 7

WEST TURRET

The West Turret

That night Lucas and Clara had a *no-sleep* sleepover.

After dinner they mapped the way to the West Turret. Then they laid out warm coats—just in case of a sudden drop in temperature—and gathered candles and candleholders.

Lucas and Clara paced eagerly, waiting for midnight to arrive. The tower bells would mark the hour.

At a quarter to midnight they put on their coats, lit their candles, and tiptoed down the passageways that led to the West Turret. The only sound was the ticking of Ruskin's long claws on the stone floor. They stopped beside a heavy oak door at the bottom of the West Turret.

"This is the wizards' chambers," Lucas whispered. Then they crept by the door and into the turret to climb up the winding stone staircase. The stairwell smelled dank and musty. Soon they came to another door.

"Okay. Now we're here," Lucas whispered. "Are you ready?"

Clara nodded. Then the prince slowly pushed the iron handle. Sticking close together, the kids and Ruskin cautiously entered the moonlit room.

The door swung shut behind them with a resounding *BAM* that boomed through the silent night. They froze, hearts racing, as the flames of their candles flickered. After a moment their fear lessened, allowing Lucas and Clara to get a better look at the room.

On one side stood a canopy bed covered in dust and cobwebs. Near the foot of the bed was a stone fireplace. The crest of Wrenly with a garland on either side was carved into the face of the mantle. A wooden

wardrobe stood next to the doorway,
and beside it was a dressing table
and chair. On top of the dressing
table lay a forgotten mirror and set
of fancy combs—all coated in a thick
layer of dust.

"Do you know who lived here?" whispered Clara.

Lucas looked out the only window. The moon danced on the waves of the sea.

"I don't know," he whispered. "The only people who come up here now are the guards on their rounds."

"Achoo!"

Ruskin sneezed, startling the kids. The poor dragon had been sniffing the soot in the fireplace. A tapestry fluttered above the mantel. Lucas held his candle higher to get a better look at the tapestry.

"This tapestry has fire-breathing dragons on it," he whispered.

Clara studied the tapestry. "Hmm, these dragons are breathing *green* fire—not red!"

Suddenly the tower bells rang,

like a warning from afar. It was midnight. Lucas and Clara looked at each other as the temperature dropped. The room became colder and colder with every chime. If the book was right, it could only mean one thing.

The ghost had arrived.

CHAPTER 8

That's the Spirit!

"Quick! Hide!" Lucas whispered.

The kids blew out their candles and scrambled into the wardrobe. Ruskin hopped in too. Through the cracked-open wardrobe door, they watched a foggy, glowing mist curl into the bedroom.

The mist took the form of a woman. She was the *exact* woman the kids had seen in the kitchen.

Both Lucas and Clara covered their mouths.

The ghost drifted to the dressing table and ran her fingers over the combs and the mirror. Then she looked around the room, searching for something. The ghost turned her gaze toward the wardrobe. Her eyes stared right at the crack in the door. The kids held still and scarcely breathed.

Then—*WHOOOOOSH!* A strong gust of wind blew in through the fireplace, making the tapestry above the mantel flutter.

This caught the ghost's attention. She studied the green fire-breathing dragons on the tapestry and floated away in surprise. Without warning, her body melted back into mist, and the ghost swished through the door and out of the room.

The children and Ruskin burst
from the wardrobe and onto the
floor.

"After her!" Lucas said in a loud
whisper.

With only the moon to light their way, the children whirled down the spiral staircase. When they reached the bottom, the mist hung right in front of the wizards' chambers.

Lucas motioned to the others, and the three of them dove back into the stairwell, out of sight. They crouched in silence and listened.

"Ahhhhhnnnnnn," wailed a voice. "Ahhhnnnndraaa."

Clara squeezed the prince's hand. "It's the ghost!"

Then the haunted voice said a name, and it was a name both the kids knew.

"ANDRÉ!"

CHAPTER 9

Kindred Spirits

Lucas peered around the corner and saw a flicker of light under the wizard's door.

"Who's there?" said a man's voice. It was André.

The ghost wailed again. "ANDRÉ! ANDRÉ!"

"Mary? Is that *you*?" The door creaked open as the old wizard peeked through the crack.

Suddenly a cold breeze shivered through the hall as the glowing mist slipped into the room through the crack in the door, which then slammed shut.

Lucas turned to Clara. "André *knows* the ghost!"

Clara's eyes were wide. "And the ghost's name is *Mary*! Do you think André was the one who wrote those notes in the margins of the book?"

"Yes," Lucas said, standing up. "He must have been tracking the ghost all along—that's why we keep bumping into him in the passageways."

Clara got up too, and she held Ruskin in place. The dragon was ready to chase the ghost.

"But why didn't André meet her in the turret at midnight?" she asked.

Lucas shrugged. "Because maybe she's not a nice, friendly ghost? Come on. Let's go."

The trio tiptoed over and pressed their ears against the door, listening to the voices inside the wizards' chambers.

"Mary, why did you come back to Wrenly Palace?" they heard André ask. "Is something the matter?"

The ghost moaned. "I am not at peace. A dream told me to find something that was hidden in *this* castle. But when I awoke, I couldn't remember what it was. I traveled the halls; checked every room; and swept through every brick, stone, and tile, searching."

André was quiet for a moment, and then he spoke. "Have you figured out what you're looking for now?"

The ghost paused. "Yes. The children have what I need."

Lucas and Clara grabbed ahold of each other.

"What do you need from *them*?" André asked.

"I need," the ghost said, "the dragon."

Lucas had heard enough. He grabbed the door handle and barged into the room.

"No one is going to lay a finger on *my* dragon!" he declared. "Especially not some haunted ghost!"

Clara and Ruskin joined the prince, ready to battle. Then André leaped between Mary and the kids.

"Everyone, settle down!" he cried.
"And please let me explain!"

The room fell quiet.

Then André began his story.
"When I was a younger wizard, I
discovered Mary's ghost in the castle,
and we became fast friends."

Mary smiled. "We are kindred spirits," she said.

André chuckled at her comment and continued. "We spent many nights talking about all things real and imagined. We discovered that magic was where our two worlds were able to meet. But then one day Mary disappeared. I searched everywhere for her but never found her until now."

Lucas looked at the wizard. "Did you ever tell anyone about Mary?"

André nodded. "Only one other," he said.

Both Lucas and
Clara looked at
each other.

"Falsk," they
both said.

André nodded again. "Indeed,
Falsk's ghost story was true. Now
Mary has returned, and she needs
our help."

Mary held out her white hands
in a welcoming way. "I need a favor
from your dragon. Rest assured, I
mean him no harm."

Lucas studied the ghost. Her kind
eyes and smile told him that she

meant well. He turned to Ruskin. The dragon nodded in agreement.

"We stand here tonight, ready to help," Lucas said.

CHAPTER 10

RIP

Mary led the way back up the turret. When they reached the forgotten room, she stood before the fireplace and addressed Ruskin.

"Here's what I need, dear dragon," she said. "It is something precious, and you must be willing to give it to me freely."

Ruskin tilted his head to one side, wondering what it could be.

Then Mary kneeled down in front of him. "What I need is some of your dragon breath."

Ruskin immediately blew a small ball of dragon fire and held it out for the ghost.

Mary laughed as if Ruskin had performed a cute puppy trick. "No, not your dragon *fire*," she said. "Your dragon *breath*."

Then Mary pointed to the green-fire-breathing dragons in the tapestry above the mantel. "I need some *green* dragon breath to light the fireplace," she explained.

This time Ruskin seemed to understand Mary's request. He stood in front of the fireplace and gently breathed on the hearth. Green sparks soon bloomed into a gentle green flame.

As the green flame flickered, the room changed. What had been dark and gloomy became light, warm, and inviting. The canopy bed came to life with fresh linen. The curtains looked clean and crisp. The mirror and combs on the dresser shone pearly white. And Mary no longer looked pale and ghostly.

Mary smiled. "Thank you, all.
You have restored my soul."

Then Mary laid on the bed and closed her eyes. And just as dew dries in the morning sun, Mary disappeared, and the gentle glow in the room faded.

The true Ghost of Wrenly would finally rest in peace.

Enter

The Kingdom of Wrenly

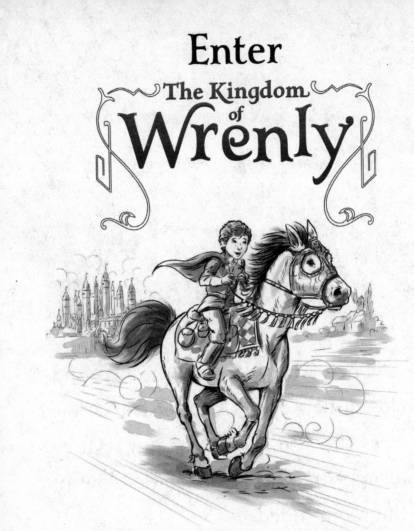

For more books, excerpts, and activities, visit

KingdomofWrenly.com!